Feelings

I'M BuSy

a Feelings Story

Clare Hibbert
Illustrated by Simona Dimitri

amicus

This title has been published with the co-operation of Cherrytree Books
Amicus Illustrated is published by Amicus
P.O. Box 1329, Mankato, Minnesota 56002

Printed in Mankato, Minnesota, USA by CG Book Printers, a division of
Corporate Graphics

Library of Congress Cataloging-in-Publication Data

Hibbert, Clare, 1970-
I'm busy : a feelings story / Clare Hibbert ; illustrated by Simona Dimitri.
    p. cm. — (Feelings)
Includes index.
ISBN 978-1-60753-176-0 (library binding)
1. Emotions in children—Juvenile literature. 2. Emotions—Juvenile literature. I.
Dimitri, Simona. II. Title.
BF723.E6H53 2011
152.4—dc22
                                                2011002241

13-digit ISBN: 978-1-60753-176-0 First Edition 1110987654321
First published in 2010 by Evans Brothers Ltd.
2A Portman Mansions, Chiltern Street, London W1U 6NR, United Kingdom

CONTENTS

Friendly

ahh!

Party

friendly

scared

busy

lonely

4

Scared

I imagined a real pirate coming to my party. I felt **scared**.

shiver

friendly

scared

busy

lonely

ahoy!

7

silly   excited   sorry   funny   special

I helped Granny make cupcakes for my party. I like being **busy**.

mix, mix!

silly

excited

sorry

funny

special

Lonely

My best friend Lily was too sick to come. She felt **lonely**.

friendly

scared

busy

lonely

I wish I could come.

silly

excited

sorry

funny

special

Silly tee hee!

friendly   scared   busy   lonely

12

silly   excited   sorry   funny   special

silly   excited   sorry   funny   special

15

Sorry

bang!

16

friendly

scared

busy

lonely

Tyler popped Anya's balloon. But he was very **sorry**.

silly

excited

sorry

funny

special

17

Funny

chuckle

18

friendly

scared

busy

lonely

The clown made everyone laugh. He was **funny**!

giggle

silly

excited

sorry

funny

special

19

Special

mwa! mwa!

friendly

scared

busy

lonely

That was the best birthday ever. I feel **special**.

silly

excited

sorry

funny

special

21

Notes for Adults

The **Feelings** series has been designed to support and extend the learning of young children. The books tie in with teaching strategies for reading with children. Find out more from the International Reading Association (www.reading.org), and The National Association for the education of Young Children (www.naeyc.org).

The **Feelings** series helps to develop children's knowledge, understanding, and skills in key social and emotional aspects of learning, in particular empathy, self-awareness, and social skills. It aims to help children understand, articulate, and manage their feelings.

Titles in the series:
I'm Happy and Other Fun Feelings looks at positive emotions
I'm Sad and Other Tricky Feelings looks at uncomfortable emotions
I'm Tired and Other Body Feelings looks at physical feelings
I'm Busy a Feelings Story explores other familiar feelings

The **Feelings** books offer the following special features:

1) **matching game**
   a border of faces gives readers the chance to hunt out the face that matches the emotion covered on the spread;
2) **fantasy scenes**
   since children often explore emotion through stories, dreams and their imaginations, two emotions (in this book, "scared" and "silly") are presented in a fantasy setting, giving the opportunity to examine intense feelings in the safety of an unreal context.

Making the most of reading time
When reading with younger children, take time to explore the pictures together. Ask children to find, identify, count, or describe different objects. Point out colors and textures. Pause in your reading so that children can ask questions, repeat your words, or even predict the next word. This sort of participation develops early reading skills.

Follow the words with your finger as you read. The main text is in Infant Sassoon, a clear, friendly font designed for children learning to read and write. The thought and speech bubbles and sound effects add fun and give the opportunity to distinguish between levels of communication.

Extend children's learning by using this book as a springboard for discussion and follow-up activities. Here are a few ideas:

Pages 4–5: Friendly

Provide paper, paints, pens, or stickers for the children to make party invitations. Encourage them to think about possible themes before they start their designs. Ask the children what information should go on the "writing side" of the invitation. Which friends would they like to invite?

Pages 6–7: Scared

Role-play being pirates. Children can raid the dress-up box or make their own eye patches, neck scarves, and toilet-roll telescopes. Sing pirate songs together. Visit http://www.singup.org/songbank/songs/view/song/66/pirates! to find the words and tune for "The pirate ship is coming."

Pages 8–9: Busy

With supervision, even young children can help bake a batch of cupcakes. They can decorate them with icing, sprinkles, and candy, or make little pirate flags like the ones in the picture.

Pages 10–11: Lonely

Talk about how the girl in the story feels. What could the boy in this story do to help his friend feel better? Can the children remember occasions when they felt lonely or left out? What helped them feel included again?

Pages 12–13: Silly

Encourage the children to practice prowling and pouncing like tigers. You could provide interesting surfaces for them to move across — for example, a bristly doormat, some crackly paper, or some child-safe sand. How quiet can the children be?

Pages 14–15: Excited

Try this guessing-game version of "Pass the Present". Wrap objects with distinctive shapes (for example, a toy dinosaur, ship and plane; a kitchen sieve, pan, and wooden spoon) in layers of old paper. Play "Pass the Present" the usual way, pausing to unwrap a layer whenever the music stops. Who can guess what's inside before the last layer of paper comes off?

Pages 16–17: Sorry

Make templates from stiff cardboard for different-sized round and long balloons. Provide paper, pencils, and safety scissors so the children can draw around the templates and cut out balloon shapes in different colors. This is a great activity for improving hand-eye coordination. Why not stick all the balloons on the wall to make an eye-catching mural?

Pages 18–19: Funny

There are lots of great games that children can play with juggling or whiffle balls. Divide children into teams and give each team a bucket and lots of small balls. Which team can throw most balls into their bucket? Count the balls together.

Pages 20–21: Special

Everyone has a birthday — their own special day. Make a big birthday calendar. Divide a big sheet of paper into 12 sections, one for each month. Make the background of each section relate to the season (for example, add ice crystals for January, puddles for February, spring flowers for March). Children can add themselves to the right months, sticking on their name and birth date, perhaps with a photo or drawing, too.

Index

Credits

The publisher would like to thank the following for permission to reproduce their images:
iStockphoto: cover and 8–9 (TerryJ), 4 envelope (leezsnow), 6–7 (Paul Cowan), 6 (GlobalP), 7 (Kangah), 8 (dcdp), 10–11 (IrvStock), 12–13 (Macsnap), 12 (ivar), 14–15 (Devonyu), 16–17 (LeggNet), 16 (JaneB), 18–19 (Gloria-Leigh), 18 (Brian A Jackson), 20 (onurdongel); **Shutterstock Images:** 4–5 (Mastering_Microstock), 4 and 14 stickers (BooHoo), 10 (Anke van Wyk), 11 (Paul Matthew Photography), 20–21 (Mark Bonham).